First American Edition 2016
Kane Miller, A Division of EDC Publishing

For information contact:
Kane Miller, A Division of EDC Publishing
P.O. Box 470663
Tulsa, OK 74147-0663

www.kanemiller.com
www.edcpub.com
www.usbornebooksandmore.com

Library of Congress Control Number: 2015960069

Printed and bound in China
1 2 3 4 5 6 7 8 9 10

ISBN: 978-1-61067-553-6

Billie's WILD JUNGLE ADVENTURE

by Sally Rippin

illustrated by Alisa Coburn

Kane Miller
A DIVISION OF EDC PUBLISHING

Billie B. Brown RUNS into preschool.

She can't wait to play
with her friends today.

"He's outside on the tire," says Miss Amy,
"swinging like a monkey."

Billie wants to swing
like a monkey too!

ooh!
ooh!
OOH!

Billie and Jack hang
from the tire, grinning
at each other.

Rustle! Rustle!

Let's go to
the jungle!

says Billie.

Together they scramble up
the mulberry tree … and
swing into the jungle.

My goodness, isn't the jungle a busy place?

"Look!" shouts Billie.
"It's the jungle-juice tree!"

Peep!
Peeeep!

Screech!

Buzzzzz!

chitter chatter

But Jack and Billie must be careful. Everyone knows that pink-and-purple pythons hide in the branches.

YUM!
says Billie.

She reaches for
a pink fruit.
Then she picks
a red one and
a yellow one.

Billie throws the fruit to Jack
and soon his hands are full.

**Watch out
for snakes!**
he says.

Billie spots a bright-
pink fruit peeking out
between the leaves.
It looks **delicious.**

up

up

She stretches ...

up

Suddenly, the fruit moves.
Oh no! It's not fruit at all.

It's a pink-and-purple python!

Billie's heart races
as the snake **winds**
and **wriggles** and
wraps itself
around her.

HiSSSSSSS?

HiSSSSSSSSS!

Uh-oh!
she thinks.

Jack's eyes grow as wide as plums.

Billie stays very still, hoping
the snake will slither away.

But just when she
thinks it might …
the snake coils up
and falls asleep!

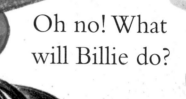

Oh no! What will Billie do?

Just then, Billie has an idea.

A **Super-duper** idea!

Throw me some fruit, she whispers to Jack.

Billie catches the fruit with
her tail and carefully holds it
up to the snake's mouth.

The snake opens an eye.
Its tongue darts out to
lick the fruit.

Billie rolls the fruit
away, just out of reach.

The snake uncoils.
It slithers along her shoulder
and onto the branch below.

Sluurp!

Billie's trick worked.
She's free!

She swings out of the tree.
Below her, a friendly tiger is
stretching on the jungle floor.
She jumps onto his back.

QUICK!

she calls to Jack.

Before the
snake sees us!

The tiger races
through the jungle,

over logs,

and under the
twisting vines.

At the bottom of the
mulberry tree, they slide
off the tiger's back.

Purrrr

"Oh no!" cries Billie. "Where's all our fruit?"
"LOOK!" says Jack.

"Cheeky monkeys!"
laughs Billie.
"Now what are
we going to eat?"

"I know," says Jack,
and he takes Billie's
arm.

They climb back up
the mulberry tree,

along the branches,
through the leaves …

... and down the tire swing.

Just in time
for fruit snack.